For my parents—S.S.W.

ACKNOWLEDGEMENTS

As I prepared this manuscript, many experts in the field of animal behavior provided valuable information and insights. I wish to thank the following who were so generous with their time:

Dr. Merlin Tuttle of Bat Conservation International, who answered many questions and checked the accuracy of the text on bats; Frank Wallace, zookeeper at the London Zoo, for a memorable visit with the rare and special animals in the Moonlight World Pavilion; Dr. Carl Shump of the University of New Hampshire, who read and discussed with me the material on mammals; Dr. Larry Harris, also of UNH, for reading the pages on marine life; Tom Arter, ornithologist, who authenticated the portion on night birds; and Dr. Frances J. White and Deborah Overdorff of the Duke University Primate Center, for information on lemurs.

Thanks also to the following who discussed many of the animals and their environments with me: Dr. Peter Siminski of the Arizona-Sonoma Museum; Rich Block of the World Wildlife Fund; Becky Suomala of the New Hampshire Audubon Society; and John Kantner of the UNH Extension Service.

SIMON & SCHUSTER BOOKS FOR YOUNG READERS, Simon & Schuster Building, Rockefeller Center, 1230 Avenue of the Americas, New York, New York 10020. Text copyright © 1993 by Susanne Santoro Whayne. Illustrations © 1993 by Steven Schindler. All rights reserved including the right of reproduction in whole or in part in any form. SIMON & SCHUSTER BOOKS FOR YOUNG READERS is a trademark of Simon & Schuster. The text of this book is set in 12 pt. Palatino. The illustrations were done in gouache on colored paper.   Manufactured in the United States of America.

10 9 8 7 6 5 4 3 2 1

Library of Congress Cataloging-in-Publication Data: Whayne, Susanne Santoro. Night Creatures / by Susanne Santoro Whayne ; illustrated by Steven Schindler.   p.   cm.   Summary: Introduces such night-active animals as cats, deer mice, toads, opossums, red foxes, fireflies, bats, and many, many more both in this and in other countries.   1. Nocturnal animals—Juvenile literature.   [1. Nocturnal animals.]   I. Schindler, S. D., ill.   II. Title. QL755.5.W53 1992 591.5—dc20 ISBN: 0-671-73395-8
91-24654
CIP

NIGHT CREATURES

by Susanne Santoro Whayne
illustrated by Steven Schindler

SIMON & SCHUSTER BOOKS FOR YOUNG READERS

Published by Simon & Schuster

New York London Toronto Sydney Tokyo Singapore

THE NIGHT SHIFT

Tonight, after you are tucked into bed, a world of animals is waking up. As you drift into dreams, night creatures are beginning their work—hunting for food, finding mates, caring for their young.

We don't usually see these *nocturnal*, or night-active, animals, but in the morning we can find signs of their visits. An overturned garbage can, a new spider web, or fresh tracks in the snow all tell us something has been busy in the night.

Why do these creatures prefer the darkness? For some it is nothing new. The first forms of life to leave the sea and live on land were probably nocturnal. Cool, damp nights protected their soft bodies. Millions of years later, most of the first mammals were nocturnal. They could not compete for food with large daytime creatures, like dinosaurs—or avoid being eaten by them! Many animals are nocturnal today for the same reasons. At night they are protected against heat and dryness; they are safe from their enemies, and they have less competition for food.

For the most part, we humans are *diurnal*, or day-active, creatures. It is easy for us to get about in the light. But how do animals manage in the dark? Many have extra-keen vision. Their huge eyes collect all possible light. Others have powerful hearing or a sense of smell that directs them as accurately as our eyes guide us. A few possess senses unknown to us—sensors that locate a prey by its body heat, or *echolocation* (ek-oh-lo-KAY-shun), a kind of sonar that guides them in total darkness.

What animals work the night shift? Night creatures can be mammals, insects, amphibians, reptiles, even birds—and some of them are right in your own neighborhood!

THE NEIGHBORHOOD

CATS

A car moves along a dark road. Caught in the headlights for a moment, two gleaming yellow eyes stare back from the roadside, then vanish into the shadows.

For thousands of years, cats have prowled the night neighborhoods. Their sensitive ears twitch and turn toward the smallest rustle. Their noses tell them what animals are nearby. And their *pupils*—the dark centers of their eyes—grow very large to collect as much light as possible. Your eyes will do this, too, in low light. But you'll never see as well as a cat, for, like those of many night creatures, cats' eyes have something extra. Behind each eye is a shiny surface, called a *tapetum* (tah-PEE-tum), that reflects light like a mirror back into the eye. This yellow or orange "eyeshine" is what we see when light catches the eye of a nocturnal animal.

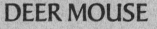

DEER MOUSE

The deer mouse rustles through the grass at night looking for insects, worms, seeds, and nuts. In the fall she will store her food in her nest inside a building or a tree stump. She belongs to the white-footed mouse family that is found throughout the United States and Europe. Mice only live a year or two in the wild, but they increase their numbers very quickly. This tiny, 1-ounce mouse had her first litter when she was just six weeks old. She will have three or four litters a year of about four babies each.

TOAD

Under the hedges, a toad waits in the darkness for an insect. He has spent the day in his burrow in the soft garden soil, and now it is time to eat. His large eyes focus best on a moving target. When something flies, crawls, or hops near him, he seizes it with a lightning-fast flick of his long, sticky tongue.

For most of the year the adult toad is a land animal; rainfall and the damp night air are enough to keep his thick skin moist. But in the spring toads make their way back to ponds to find mates. The tadpoles take only three to four weeks to develop in the water. By summer the young toads are ready to find their homes on land.

RACCOON

While many animals are endangered today, four night creatures are flourishing. Raccoons, skunks, opossums, and foxes are all successful because they can live almost anywhere and eat almost anything. Their dens and hunting grounds may be quite close to humans, yet their nocturnal habits keep them out of sight.

Raccoons are at home in cities, suburbs, and the countryside, from Canada to Central America. They can swim, climb, and fight off big dogs. Their five fingers are always busy digging, probing, and examining. A closed cabinet or fastened trash can is not much of a challenge to the wily raccoon!

Raccoons match their diet to the seasons. In the spring they raid nests for eggs and young animals. Their summer menu includes wild greens, frogs, and crayfish. Fall is the time to fatten up on nuts, berries, and insects. Their fat will keep them warm throughout their long winter naps in tree hollows or vacant buildings.

SKUNK

An unmistakable fragrance fills the night air. The slow-moving skunk has only one weapon, but that is usually all he needs! Under his tail are the ends of two musk glands that the skunk can direct up, down, and sideways.

A skunk gives warning before he sprays. He stamps his front feet and arches his tail. If that doesn't work, he turns and shoots his scent up to 12 feet. Skunks also use their odor for communicating. A lingering scent marks their territory, and a light whiff in the darkness helps a family keep track of each other. In less-friendly moments, skunks will spray each other in quarrels over food.

During the day the skunk nestles in his underground burrow. At night he searches for food, which ranges from spring snakes and summer grasshoppers to fall fruit. His favorites, however, are mice and insects. Although you might have to hold your nose when he's in the neighborhood, the skunk is a very useful animal.

OPOSSUM

All night long the opossum forages the neighborhood. In her search for mice, earthworms, insects, or road kill, she might cover over a mile. The young mother opossum does not need to bother with trips back to a den. Her young travel with her, for the opossum is North America's only *marsupial*, or pouched animal. The babies are born hairless, blind, and deaf. They are so tiny that an entire litter of fourteen weighs less than an ounce and can fit inside a bottle cap! The newborns complete their development in their mother's pouch. After about a hundred days, they crawl out of her pouch and ride on her back.

Thirty-five million years ago, the first opossums wandered up from South America. Today, their numbers and range are still spreading. Even in northern states, where few can survive a second winter, the gentle, persistent opossum seeks out a home under buildings, in hollow trees, or in heavy brush.

RED FOX

At the edge of a clearing, a fox crouches motionless for a moment, listening. Then, in a graceful arc, he leaps on his prey, a cottontail rabbit. Although foxes belong to the dog family, they hunt more like cats—stealthily, by surprise attack, and alone.

This male fox, or *dog*, started his hunting at dusk with a feast of earthworms, beetles, and grubs. Sometimes, when a fox finds more food than he can eat, he will *cache* (KASH), or hide, the surplus. He digs a shallow hole, pushes the food in with his nose, then carefully covers up the hiding place. His sense of smell will lead him back to the cache when food is less available. But this fox has pups back at his den. For the litter's first $3\frac{1}{2}$ months, the dog and his mate, the *vixen*, bring them food. In the fall the pups will find their own dens. One or two females may remain with the parents and help them raise next year's pups.

Although we may think of foxes as country creatures, they adapt well to towns and suburbs. They dig their burrows in railroad banks, parks, or cemeteries.

THE SKIES AT NIGHT

MOTHS

On summer nights tiny wings beat at the window screen and circle the porch light. Why are these insects drawn to the light? One way a moth guides itself is by aligning its eyes to the moon. It stays on course with little turns to keep its body at a fixed angle to the moon's rays. When it circles a light bulb, it acts in the same way. But now, each turn brings it closer to the light; and instead of flying straight, the moth spirals right into the bulb.

The tiger moth is a familiar night visitor. Her bright colors remind enemies of her unpleasant taste.

FIREFLIES

Fireflies have a unique way of finding each other at night. When darkness falls, they call to each other with twinkling lights. We usually see the male as he signals from the air with two tiny lanterns under his body. The female, which cannot fly, is harder to spot. She crawls to the end of a stalk and answers with her own light. The length of the male's flashing tells her that this is one of her own species. And so, led by a kind of Morse code in lights, a meeting is arranged.

WHIPPOORWILL

With the rising of the moon, *whippoorwill* cries begin. Over and over again, at the rate of one per second, the whippoorwill calls, telling other birds, "This is my territory." One hundred straight calls are not unusual. An especially vocal whippoorwill might serenade the countryside with sixteen thousand calls in one night! It is easy to understand why members of this family, which jar the night, are called "nightjars" in Europe.

When his song has finally ended, the whippoorwill flies low to the ground, eating mosquitoes and moths on the wing. Bristlelike feathers around his mouth help to snare the insects.

Whippoorwills do not build nests but lay their two eggs right on the leafy forest floor. The nesting pair is camouflaged by their speckled coloring. And because they are night hunters, there is no daytime activity to alert their enemies.

OWLS

The whippoorwill's song is one of the few you will hear after sunset. Most birds cannot see well enough, even by moonlight, to feed at night. One bird, however, dominates the darkness. No other night bird—and few night animals—can match the owl's keen senses or the dead accuracy of her hunting.

Only a haunting hoot lets us know she's there. Her approach is silent; the fringed edges of her feathers muffle the sound of her flight. The owl is guided by her powerful night vision. Her eyes are so huge that there is no room in her head for muscles to turn them. Instead, the owl rotates her entire head—almost three-quarters of the way around.

Even more amazing is an owl's hearing. It is so sharp that some owls, like the barn owl, can hunt in complete darkness. The bowl-shaped feathers around the owl's eyes collect and direct sound to her ears like a satellite dish. Her ear openings are at the sides of her head, and some owls have one opening higher than the other. In this way, the owl can tell not only the side from which the sound is coming but also whether the source is above or below her.

Owls, which often mate for life, take good care of their young. The male supplies the nest with fresh game; and both parents defend the nest fiercely, especially after the young hatch. The fledglings leave the nest before they can fly. One by one the young birds drop to the ground, then rush to climb a nearby tree. The parents continue to watch over the young for several months, until they can fly about and hunt on their own.

SCREECH OWL

Most owls live and hunt in the woods or open countryside. Screech owls, however, do not seem to mind the noise and activity of a neighborhood. They are small owls—about the size of robins—and they find plenty of insects, rodents, and small snakes in yards and wooded lots. But because they swoop low to the ground as they hunt, one of the greatest dangers they face is a collision with a car.

BARN OWL

In some countries the handsome barn owl is called the "monkey-faced owl." By any name, a barn owl, with her great appetite for rats, is welcomed by farmers in Europe, Asia, and Africa.

Barn owls do not bother with nest-building. They lay their five to seven eggs in a high, flat, sheltered place—on a ledge, in a barn loft, or in a church steeple. As with many other owls, the eggs will hatch over several days. The first eggs laid are the first to hatch. This means that the brood will always have some older and stronger chicks. If food is scarce, the bigger chicks have the best chance for survival.

GREAT HORNED OWL

The great horned owl, with his magnificent 5-foot wingspan, is one of North America's largest owls. He is a fierce hunter that preys on rabbits, opossums, mice, and smaller owls. He will also take young raccoons and even an occasional cat. If you were wondering whether skunks have any natural enemies, they do. The great horned owl is one of the very few creatures to hunt skunks, and his feathers and nest often have the odor to prove it!

BATS

For hundreds of years, bats have been misunderstood and feared. Storytellers have frightened their audiences by linking these gentle night creatures with demons and disease—and bats have suffered because of it. Millions of bats have been killed, and today many species are extinct or close to it. Yet these shy insect-eaters are enormously helpful to the environment and are special in many ways.

Bats are the only mammal that can fly. A bat's wings are actually his hands. In his thin, almost transparent wing membrane you can see a bat's four fingers and thumb. Bats use their wings like hands—to scoop insects into their mouths, to cradle their young, and to comfort another bat that is sick or cold.

Bats have mastered flight without sight. Although they use their good eyesight when light is available, they can also navigate, even in total darkness, by using echolocation. A bat sends out a series of squeaks that bounce off an object. The echoes return to tell him where the target is. Since many bats, and their targets, move fast, their squeaks must be fast, too. A bat may send out 10 squeaks a second as he approaches an object and up to *200* a second as he zeroes in on it. You may have seen pictures of open-mouthed bats, which look quite menacing. But the bats are not snarling, they are just echolocating. Some bats send out squeaks with their noses instead of their mouths. This allows them to navigate with their mouths full!

FREE-TAILED BAT

Huge numbers of free-tailed bats roost together in caves throughout the year. Twenty million free-tails live in the Bracken Cave in central Texas. They are the largest colony of wild mammals in the world. Each twilight, the bats leave the cave. Their departure fills the skies with bats for three hours. By morning the bats return, after eating an amazing *quarter million pounds* of insects!

A bat takes very good care of the one pup she bears each year. Free-tailed babies roost in a nursery area on the cave's ceiling. The pups are packed tightly together—as many as five thousand in a 3-foot-by-3-foot area—and are kept warm by body heat. Yet, even among the millions of bats in the cave, a mother has no trouble finding her own pup. After a few calls and answers, the mother makes a beeline for her pup, gathers him up with her wing, and nurses him until he is full.

LITTLE BROWN BAT

The little brown bat can be found in most parts of the United States. Like all bats from cool climates in North America, Europe, and Asia, she is an insect-eater with a big appetite. Some nights, she may eat up to half her body weight in insects; and if she is nursing a pup, she may eat her *entire* weight in insects. (This would be like you eating a 100-pound supper!) During the summer little brown bats roost in trees, caves, or buildings. In autumn they hibernate in caves. A bat is most at risk during hibernation. If disturbed, she will awaken; but she will use two to four weeks' worth of her precious store of fat to bring up her body to its normal temperature. Without enough stored fat to last the winter, the bat will surely starve.

BEAVERS

Out in the country lives a family of hard-working night creatures. Every evening, the beavers inspect their dam and check the water level. When repairs are needed, the family pitches in to help. The older beavers haul branches and grass. They dive for mud and stones, then pat them into place with their monkeylike hands. The four kits from this year's litter are still too young for real work, but they watch and practice towing branches.

Once this was a forest with a flowing stream, but the beavers have made big changes. With sharp rodent teeth, they gnawed down hardwood trees to dam the brook and create the pond. Now there are frogs and fish in the water and ducks nesting in the reeds. The pond is a watering hole for deer, moose, raccoons, and foxes, and a rest stop for migrating geese.

Beavers are perfectly suited for their lives in the pond. Their sleek fur is waterproof, and their broad back feet are webbed. Their tails act like rudders as they cruise the pond at a brisk 5 mph, and they are able to stay underwater for as long as twenty minutes. Transparent membranes protect their eyes. They can shut their ears and nostrils tightly. They can seal off their throats, too, so they can bite off underwater branches without gagging.

The sociable beavers have learned the secret of working and living in harmony. The family is headed by parents that stay together all their lives. The yearlings from last year's litter work in the pond and help care for the new kits. The family may even welcome back older offspring that couldn't find their own homes.

At summer's end the beavers turn their attention to fixing up their lodge. This dome-shaped building, made of grass and woven twigs, will be the family's cozy winter home. The outside is finished with a coat of mud that freezes to a hard plaster. Inside is a sturdy floor with two exit holes and 3 or 4 feet of headroom. Near the exits is an underwater stockpile of branches to feed on during the winter.

Someday, the beavers will use up the supply of trees near the pond and move to a new brook. When that happens, the abandoned dam will give way eventually and the pond will drain. Grasses will sprout on the rich, damp soil, and the old pond will become a meadow home for new kinds of life. Pheasant, rabbits, and mice will make their homes in the tall grasses, and owls and foxes will hunt them. Perhaps, in time, new trees will take root, and this will once again be a forest with a flowing stream.

COYOTE

In Native American legends, the coyote is a clever trickster that outsmarts the other animals. Today, the coyote needs his cunning more than ever. He has been hunted persistently by farmers and ranchers who fear his nighttime raids on their livestock. Yet the coyote still flourishes. It is hard to discourage coyotes, but easy to admire them. As soon as traps and poison are set out, coyotes learn where they are and how to avoid them. Coyotes are just as clever at finding homes. They easily adapt to different environments and have settled throughout North America, on prairies and deserts, and in mountains and forests.

Coyotes are skillful hunters with excellent sight, smell, and hearing. When hunting deer and other large animals, these members of the dog family work as a pack, taking turns chasing the prey until it is exhausted. Coyotes hunt alone for small game, like mice, snakes, and gophers. Their 40-mph running speed is fast enough to capture one of their favorites, the snowshoe hare.

ARMADILLO

Grunting and sniffing, an odd-looking creature noses through a Texas field. His head, back, and tail are covered with rows of bony plates. This shining armor in the night belongs to the armadillo. He's an insect-eater that can smell grubs half a foot under the soil. When his nose locates something tasty, he furiously rakes the dirt with his sharp front claws. Sometimes his digging habits get him into trouble with gardeners, but his appetite for harmful insects makes him more friend than pest.

The timid armadillo does not like to be far from his burrow. When he senses danger, he makes a dash for home. If that is not possible, he may swim away. He gulps air to keep himself afloat. If all else fails, he jumps straight up in the air. Unfortunately, many armadillos do this on the highway, which is disastrous when cars pass over them. The armadillo's most amazing ability belongs to the female. The mother-to-be can delay delivering her babies for up to $2\frac{1}{2}$ years! This allows her to wait out droughts or move to a better food supply. It may also have been helpful when armadillos began to travel north from Mexico about 150 years ago.

SNOWSHOE HARE

On summer nights a grayish-brown snowshoe hare ventures out of the underbrush to nibble grasses and clover. In autumn, as her body senses the days shortening, her fur begins to fall out. Over the next ten weeks her coat grows in much lighter, and by winter she is all white. Now she travels across the snow on her wide, snowshoelike back feet, nearly invisible to predators. Her ability to change her wardrobe with the seasons gives her the nickname "varying hare."

Because they are so often hunted by owls and coyotes, few snowshoes survive beyond two years. But hares, like rabbits, reproduce quickly. Two or three litters are born each year. The three to six babies, called *leverets*, weigh only $2\frac{1}{2}$ ounces at birth; yet they are completely furry, and their eyes are open. After only six or seven weeks, the young hares hop off to live on their own.

SOUTHERN FLYING SQUIRREL

Out in the forest at dusk, an animal sails from tree to tree. He is airborne, but not a bird; he is furry, but not a bat. Although called a flying squirrel, he really is not flying. He is gliding. Sometimes, if he catches an air current, he travels over 100 feet! To launch himself, the flying squirrel makes a kind of kite out of his body, spreads his arms, stretching tightly the flaps of skin between his front and back feet, then pushes off with his back legs and soars through the branches.

These long glides are made possible by the flying squirrels' incredibly light weight. The 6-inch southern flying squirrel weighs less than 3 ounces. Flying squirrels live in North America, Europe, and Asia. They are active throughout the year, and are quite sociable. During the day, especially in cold weather, they cluster together in hollow trees or abandoned woodpecker holes.

WHITE-TAILED DEER

Under the cover of darkness, a deer moves cautiously through the trees. Every few minutes she stops to listen, sniff the breeze, and peer into the shadows. If she detects a sound, a scent, or a movement, she freezes for a moment, blending in with the foliage. Then she lifts her tail, showing a flash of white fur, and bounds off.

Deer have many enemies. Darkness, alert senses, and the ability to make a quick escape are their safeguards. Making little noise, adult deer usually travel alone, feeding on leaves, bark, nuts, and wild fruits. Newborn fawns are especially vulnerable. Their protection lies in their camouflage coloring and their lack of scent.

Only male deer have antlers, and they grow a new set each spring. The tender new antlers are covered with a layer of soft skin and hair called *velvet*. When the antlers are full-size, the buck rubs against trees to remove the velvet. In the fall bucks use their antlers to gain the attention of does and, once they have it, to warn off other bucks. In winter, after the mating season, the buck's antlers drop off. They have served their purpose for the bucks, and now they help squirrels and mice. These little animals, in need of winter food, gnaw eagerly at the mineral-rich antlers.

GRAY WOLF

Deep in the Canadian wilderness a howl breaks the night's silence. Before the cry ends another begins. Soon a chorus of wolf howls fills the air, rising, falling, and ending in a series of yips and yaps.

Why do wolves howl? Often the cries, which can be heard 5 miles away, are saying, "This is our hunting ground—stay away!" Protecting its territory is very important to a wolf pack. Wolves are the largest members of the dog family. Each may weigh over 100 pounds and eat 4 to 8 pounds of meat a day. To keep a pack of fifteen wolves healthy, they need to kill a deer or moose every two days.

Sometimes wolves invade another pack's territory. Then the howls announce, "Here we come!" The home pack may find it easier to retreat than to risk injuries or death in a fight. But if there are pups they can't move or a kill they won't abandon, the pack may stand its ground.

Wolves hunt by teamwork. Each seems to know what the other is doing, and what he will do next. A typical hunt begins as one or two wolves scout out the prey, perhaps a herd of caribou. Keeping downwind, the scouts determine which caribou can be taken. The prey, often a sick or old animal, is quickly surrounded and run in circles until it falls. If a longer chase is needed, the tireless wolves have the advantage. The pack can run 20 miles in a night and have been known to cover 125 miles in twenty-four hours!

These ferocious hunters show a very different side when they are caring for their young. The head male, called the *alpha*, and his mate produce the pups, but all the adults help care for them. The father and his older sons and daughters take turns "baby-sitting" while the mother hunts. Daytime hours are spent patiently playing with the litter and watching them explore. The pups play-fight over bones and scraps and practice their hunting skills by pouncing on insects. The young wolves, born in April, will be nearly full-grown by fall. They will stay with the pack three years or more.

Gray wolves once roamed throughout the cool forests of North America, Europe, and Asia. In Asia they still prowl the steppes. In North America the howl of the gray wolf is now heard only in Alaska, Canada, and the northern border states of the United States.

THE TROPICAL RAIN FOREST

Thousands of miles south of wolf country is a very different kind of forest. In the tropical rain forest, trees grow more than 100 feet high to reach the sunlight. Their crowns are so close together that they form a leafy umbrella. The light is filtered down through layers of leaves, vines, and brilliant flowers. Under its green canopy, the forest floor is dim, even during the day. The low light keeps the floor mostly open and free of undergrowth.

A huge variety of animal life flourishes in this warm, humid environment. In fact, the rain forests of South and Central America, Madagascar, Africa, and Indonesia are home to half of all the earth's animal and plant species. The thick foliage teems with activity. Like busy high-rise apartment dwellers, many animals make their homes in the trees and go about their daily, and nightly, tasks there.

ASIAN CLIMBING TOAD

Night falls quickly in the tropics. As the last birdsong fades with the light, toads and frogs emerge from the leaves and add their voices to the hum of insects. These tree-dwelling amphibians have sticky pads at the ends of their wide-tipped toes to help them climb tree limbs and trunks. The beautifully colored Asian climbing toad is only 4 inches long. The females attract their mates with their vivid colors. The males are a drab brownish-black.

ASIAN FLYING FROG

When he hunts insects on the ground, the 3-inch Asian flying frog does not waste time. He pushes off from his perch high in the tree and glides to the ground 50 feet below. Because of the moist air, many tropical frogs and toads do not need to live in a pond. They drink water that collects in trees and find a stream or pool only when it is time to lay their eggs.

KIWI

Not all the rain forest action is in the trees. On the forest floor a kiwi bird pokes through the leaves looking for earthworms and insects. Her long, flexible bill has nostrils at the tip for sniffing out food on the ground. The kiwi is a fast runner and a good jumper. But even though she has little wings hidden in her hairlike feathers, there is one thing she cannot do—fly. The kiwi lives only in New Zealand. In her island home she does not have the natural enemies that would make quick work of a small, flightless bird.

TOKAY GECKO

From a vine-twisted branch, a gecko gives its *to-kay* call. He is a friendly insect-eater. In India, Indonesia, and the Philippines, the gecko is sometimes taken into homes as a pet. There he will scurry up and down the walls in his night-long hunt for insects and spiders. The little suction cups on his toe pads work so well that a gecko can even travel up and down panes of glass.

SLENDER LORIS

The slender loris creeps through the branches on skinny legs. She is searching for geckos. When she spots one, she makes a grab with her front paws and kills the lizard with well-placed bites. Her back feet look and act like pincers. She uses them to grip thin branches and to groom her fur. After a night of hunting in the forests of Sri Lanka, the slender loris returns to the higher branches, where she curls into a ball, almost invisible in the foliage, and sleeps the day away.

BUSH BABY

Bush babies are East African cousins of the slender loris. These curious, affectionate creatures are spectacular jumpers. Although their silky-furred bodies are only a foot tall, they can leap 25 feet from tree to tree! On the ground they hop upright, like kangaroos, with their long tails straight behind them. Bush babies' big ears give them super-sharp hearing. They can also rotate their ears to direct their hearing. And when they are ready to sleep, the little bush babies give themselves some peace and quiet by folding up their ears like fans.

PANGOLIN

In the tropics of central Africa, termites build huge, cone-shaped homes, some more than 10 feet high. Where there is a termite colony, there is likely to be a hungry pangolin. Using his strong front claws, he rips through the mound and scoops up termites with his sticky, foot-long tongue. If the termites fight back, the pangolin's hard, overlapping scales protect him. He can also close his nostrils and ear openings, squeeze shut his thick eyelids, and shake the insects off.

The only vulnerable part of a pangolin is his soft belly. To protect himself completely, he rolls into a tight ball and, for good measure, gives off a foul smell!

On the ground, a pangolin moves slowly and awkwardly, often on his back legs. Because of his long, curved back claws, he must walk on the outside edges of his feet. But he's quite comfortable in a tree, sometimes hanging from a branch by his tail.

LEMURS

If you want to see a lemur in his natural home, you have only one place to look. All the lemurs in the world live in Madagascar, an island off the southeastern coast of Africa. Scientists aren't sure how the lemurs got there. Their ancestors may have been in the area when it broke off from the mainland millions of years ago and gradually drifted 240 miles offshore. Or they may have crossed the water on their own, riding on logs and branches. We do know that they left behind on the continent many mammals that would have been tough competition for them. Isolated in Madagascar, the lemurs flourished. Once there were more than forty different species, including some 100- and 200-pound giants. But rain forests, and the animals that live in them, are disappearing at a frightening rate—worldwide, we lose *42 million acres each year.* Today in Madagascar, only 16 percent of the original rain forest remains, and just twenty-eight lemur species survive.

Lemurs are members of the primate family, which means they share a common ancestor with monkeys, apes, and us, if we trace our lines back 50 million years or so. The lemurs' branch of the family is called prosimian (pro-SIM-ee-an). They are the "lower," or less-developed, primates. You may notice their family resemblance to other prosimians—the lorises and bush babies.

MOUSE LEMUR

Since lemurs evolved apart from many other creatures, some of them have taken on the roles of other animals found in different parts of the world. The tiny mouse lemur has the size and habits of a rodent. She lives on fruits and insects like a mouse, and she climbs trees and jumps from branch to branch like a squirrel.

The mouse lemur eats heartily in the four-month rainy season when food is plentiful. Her body grows quite chubby then, especially her tail. When the rains stop and water and food are scarce, she lives off her stored fat. During the hottest, driest season, the mouse lemur curls up in her grass- and leaf-lined nest and goes to sleep. This long, inactive period during warm weather resembles hibernation and is called *aestivation* (es-teh-VAY-shun).

The mouse lemur is one of the world's smallest primates. She weighs no more than an egg, and would fit in the palm of your hand with room to spare.

AYE-AYE

A first glimpse of the aye-aye, with his eerie grin and strange, skeletal hands, might startle you. But for many Madagascan natives it's worse than that—it's terrifying! Many believe that whoever the aye-aye points to is marked for death. In some villages it is forbidden to harm an aye-aye, but in others he is killed on sight.

In reality, the aye-aye is a rare, cat-sized lemur with the behavior and diet of a woodpecker. He uses his long, bony fingers for very practical purposes. First he locates beetle larvae by tapping on bamboo canes or decayed trees. His hearing is so keen he can detect movement inside the wood. Once the grubs are located, the aye-aye chews through the bark with his sharp teeth. Then he digs the insects out with his wire-thin middle finger. He squeezes the morsels into a juicy pulp and, like a satisfied diner, licks his fingers when he is done!

33

FLYING FOXES

After the birds have gone to roost and the butterflies have folded their wings, pale night flowers open in the moonlight. These are bat flowers, and their strong scent calls to the bats from up to a mile away.

The bats that feed in the night gardens are called "flying foxes." They dart among the blossoms like dark birds, lapping up nectar and pollen. One hundred and seventy species of flying foxes live in Southeast Asia, central and south Africa, and on islands in the Pacific and Indian oceans. They are the main pollinators of many night-blooming plants, such as the banana and baobab trees.

These foxy-faced bats are vegetarians. Since their targets do not move, the bats never developed echolocation. Instead, they navigate with excellent night vision and a keen sense of smell.

Flying foxes also feed on soft, ripe fruit. They squeeze the fruit to a pulp with their teeth. As they travel, the bats spread the seeds in their droppings. In this way wild bananas, mangoes, dates, and many other species are re-seeded.

Without tropical bats, many species of plants might perish. This loss would then endanger the animals that feed on the plants and are sheltered by them. In a kind of tragic chain reaction, the decreased numbers of these animals would in turn threaten other animals and plants.

TENT-MAKING BATS

Most tropical bats find daytime shelter in trees or caves. Some of the leaf-nosed bats of Central and South America, however, prefer a cozier, homemade roost. They build their own "tents" from the leaves. These small bats chew halfway through the ribs of the undersides of leaves. The leaf folds down, but just enough of the vein remains to keep it attached and alive. To roost, the bat hooks his feet on to the ribs and hangs head down in his own little tent. Now the bat has a shelter that keeps him shaded and dry, hidden from enemies, and protected from the wind.

THE AFRICAN SAVANNA

The African savanna is the last of the world's great pastures. The grasslands begin south of the Sahara. They stretch thousands of miles across the continent, skirt the rain forests of central Africa, and continue on to southern Africa. Scattered throughout the savannas are clumps of trees, winding rivers, and marshy water holes. Herds of zebras, giraffes, wildebeests, and gazelles graze here, keeping a sharp watch for predators. In the daylight lions and cheetahs stalk the herds. But night is the leopards' time.

LEOPARD

The leopard is a silent, solitary hunter. Although he can weigh up to 200 pounds, he stalks his prey through the tall grass without a sound. Often he strikes by ambush. He watches from a tree branch. His night vision is so sharp that he can see in almost total darkness. When his prey is within striking distance, the leopard leaps and pounces. Almost before the victim realizes what has happened, the leopard has knocked it down and fastened his fangs on its neck.

The leopard hunts most of the grazing animals, as well as baboons, warthogs, and wild dogs; and he doesn't leave scraps for the scavengers. When he has eaten his fill, he carries the leftovers up into a tree, out of the reach of jackals and hyenas.

Leopards are the most widespread of the big cats. They can be found in the rain forests, the mountains of India, and the highlands of China. They are still endangered in many areas; however, protection from hunters and fur trappers has helped increase their numbers. Today in Africa there are at least 700,000 of these graceful, night-hunting cats.

HIPPOPOTAMUS

At sunset the hippopotamuses leave the rivers to graze on the grass of the savanna. Their powerful shoulder muscles pull their 4-ton bodies up onto the riverbanks. They will graze all night, traveling as far as 5 miles. By dawn they will each have eaten as much as 150 pounds of grass! The hippos leave the grassland in early morning, but they don't stop eating for long. They spend the day in the water, feeding on water cabbage.

The females and their young live together in peaceful groups of about fifteen. The young hippo, which was a 100-pound newborn, stays close to his mother, sometimes resting on her back. Each male, however, stakes out his territory. He warns off invaders by showing his 12-inch tusks.

Hippopotamuses move gracefully in the water, swimming and walking on the bottom along underwater paths. The weight of their bodies keeps them submerged. When they rest, they can still breathe and keep watch. Their nostrils, eyes, and ears are at the top of their head, just above the waterline.

THE DESERT

As soon as the fiery desert sun sets, night creatures leave their underground burrows and sheltered nests to find food. The days here can be brutal, even in the wooded canyons. The sun blazes down, heating the air to over 100 degrees Fahrenheit. The rainfall averages only a few inches a year. Most creatures would overheat and *dehydrate*, or dry out, in just a few daytime hours. Yet, almost one-fifth of the earth's surface is desert; and it is home to mammals, reptiles, and birds. To survive, these creatures have adapted to life in the dark.

MERRIAM KANGAROO RAT

If you see a kangaroo rat make a fast getaway, you will know how she got her name. She doesn't run, she hops on her long hind legs. She also uses her tail like a kangaroo does—to balance her when she is moving fast, and to prop her up when she sits.

The kangaroo rat never drinks. She gets all the moisture she needs from her diet of seeds and juicy roots. Since she doesn't sweat, she loses very little liquid. In the fall the kangaroo rat dries seeds in the hot sand so they won't get moldy. Then she carries them in her cheeks to her underground burrow for winter storage. The Merriam, from the western United States and Mexico, is the smallest kangaroo rat. Her body is only 4 inches long, but her tail adds another 6 inches. She weighs less than 2 ounces.

ELF OWL

The spring return of the elf owls to the Sonoma Desert is the noisiest time of the year. Like excited vacationers, happy to be back and full of news, they rouse the desert night with their whistles and barklike calls.

Their first job is to find a home. Almost any little niche will do. The size of sparrows and weighing less than an ounce, the elf owls are the smallest North American owls. Many of them will nest in the holes woodpeckers have bored in saguaro cacti. Once the owls have paired off and settled in, they quietly raise their young.

Although they are tiny, elf owls are not timid. They often visit neighborhoods, flying around porch lights to hunt for moths. In October they leave Arizona and New Mexico to spend the winter in western Mexico.

SIDEWINDER

The sidewinder also has a unique way of traveling, which gives him his name. He forms his body into two S-shaped loops and moves by throwing the loops diagonally forward. Only the bends of his looped body actually touch the ground—a good idea in hot, loose sand.

The sidewinder is a member of the pit viper family from the southwestern United States. These poisonous snakes find their targets like heat-sensing missiles. Sensors in the pits between their nose and eyes detect anything that is even just the slightest bit warmer than the air. Sidewinders track mice and lizards through the cool night air, sometimes right into their burrows.

39

FENNEC FOX

The fennec fox emerges from his burrow in the Sahara Desert and listens for a moment to the night sounds. He is a shy, nervous creature; and at the first sign of danger, he will dash for cover.

As you might guess from his huge ears, the fennec fox hunts mainly by hearing. He can detect the faintest rustle from an insect, rodent, or lizard. Those oversized ears also help him keep cool, as they provide a lot of surface to radiate heat from his body.

WOMBAT

The surface of the Australian desert is barren and lifeless. The dry, caked earth is scattered with rocks and scruffy plants. But 10 feet underground the wombats have created an amazing landscape. Their burrow, up to 100 feet long, contains a series of passageways, chambers, and more than twenty exits. There are nursery rooms for mothers and babies, and individual bachelor quarters for the adults. As many as fifteen wombats may live here peacefully. The burrow also provides shelter for other desert animals; rabbits, snakes, and birds all seek out its coolness.

An underground home is a wombat's solution to the scorching summers and the frigid winters of an Australian desert. His burrow is an even, moist, 70 degrees Fahrenheit. In this land of frequent droughts, the wombat may go without drinking for more than fifteen years! Like the kangaroo rat, he takes his moisture from his food, and the damp air helps his body retain it.

Wombats are chubby marsupials, measuring 3 feet long and weighing about 60 pounds. For many years they were thought to be digging pests, and hunters were paid for killing them. Their numbers are still threatened today, as they are very slow to reproduce. Females do not give birth until they are three years old, and then they will have only one baby a year.

THE SHORE: GHOST CRABS, PERIWINKLES, AND GREEN SEA TURTLES

The seashore is quieter at night. By day the sharp-eyed gulls hunt the shores, their cries a reminder of their appetites. At night, however, when the temperature falls and the air becomes damp, many small, soft-bodied creatures are safe from the sun and the birds.

Ghost crabs scurry from their daytime hiding places in the sand. Running sideways, with their claws folded in front, they find the high-water line. They are beachcombers that will spend the night picking through seaweed and beach debris, and feeding on sand fleas, dead fish, and perhaps a leftover sandwich or two.

On the rocks, periwinkles stretch out of their shells. Their soft bodies would have dried out quickly in the sun. Now, in the moist night air, they creep over the rocks to feed on algae and bits of seaweed.

Huge domed shells, 4 to 5 feet across, rise out of the waves at the water's edge. The green sea turtles are coming ashore to lay their eggs. On tropical beaches, from October to February, the females spend nearly all night in the process. The enormous, 300-pound turtles slowly make their way to the sands above the high-tide mark. Each one finds a spot and, using her front flippers, makes a shallow pit for her body. Then, with her back flippers, she digs a hole and deposits her 50 to 100 eggs. After she covers the nest with sand, her mothering is finished, and she returns to the waters.

After six or seven weeks the sea turtles hatch, but they must wait for night to leave their nest. If they emerge during the day, the little turtles, with their soft shells, will be easy targets for the gulls. Somehow they know, perhaps by the drop in temperature, when night falls and it is time to push out of the sand and race to the water. Not all of them will make it, for in close pursuit will be the ghost crabs.

IN THE WATERS: LANTERN FISH, FLASHLIGHT FISH, VIPER FISH, FLYING FISH, WANDERING ALBATROSS

Out in the ocean, nighttime brings a changing of the guard. The daytime fish, which feed close to the surface, retreat to lower waters. Taking their places are the deepwater fish. They rise to the surface to prey on shrimp and smaller fish.

Here and there the dark waves are broken by strange glows and blinking lights. Many of the night creatures are *bioluminescent* (BY-oh-loo-meh-NES-sent), which means they create their own light. Their light helps them lure their prey, for shrimp and other small creatures are attracted to light, much like moths. The light may also be used to startle bigger fish and provide a quick getaway. Still other fish use light to signal to their own kind, like fireflies in a field.

The 3-inch lantern fish wears a row of glowing lights on his stomach. He travels to the surface from his daytime home 1,000 feet below the North Atlantic Ocean.

Flashlight fish from the Red Sea can switch their lights off and on. The small but intense beams come from bean-shaped light organs just below their eyes. Covering the organs is a membrane that the fish can blink open and shut.

The deep-sea viper fish casts for her dinner with a glowing line. She is a deadly, foot-long predator that rises from the depths more than a mile below the surface. She has been known to take on, and somehow swallow, fish larger than herself!

In a sudden burst, a flying fish leaps from the water. He is escaping the hungry jaws of a dolphin fish. With fins held straight out, he rises 3 feet into the air and glides over the waves. If he catches the wind just right, he can glide the length of two football fields before he puts down.

A wandering albatross scans the waters looking for squid and fish. Her immense wings, up to 12 feet across, let her soar without flapping for several minutes. When she spots a prey, she swoops down and plucks it from the waves. The albatross is a creature of the wind and water. She touches land—an island in the South Atlantic or Pacific—only when it is time to breed. Both parents take turns sitting on the single egg and help feed the chick for the next year.

It has been a busy night on the ocean. Soon it will be dawn and time for the day shift. In the waters, and in the forests and deserts, the sun will send the night creatures back to their daytime resting places. Not far from your home the cats will return to their porches, the skunks and foxes will find their burrows, and the bats will go back to their roosts. As you rise from your bed, a world of animals is going to sleep. Now is your time to enjoy the day; and while you do, the night creatures will be tucked away, waiting their turn in the neighborhood.